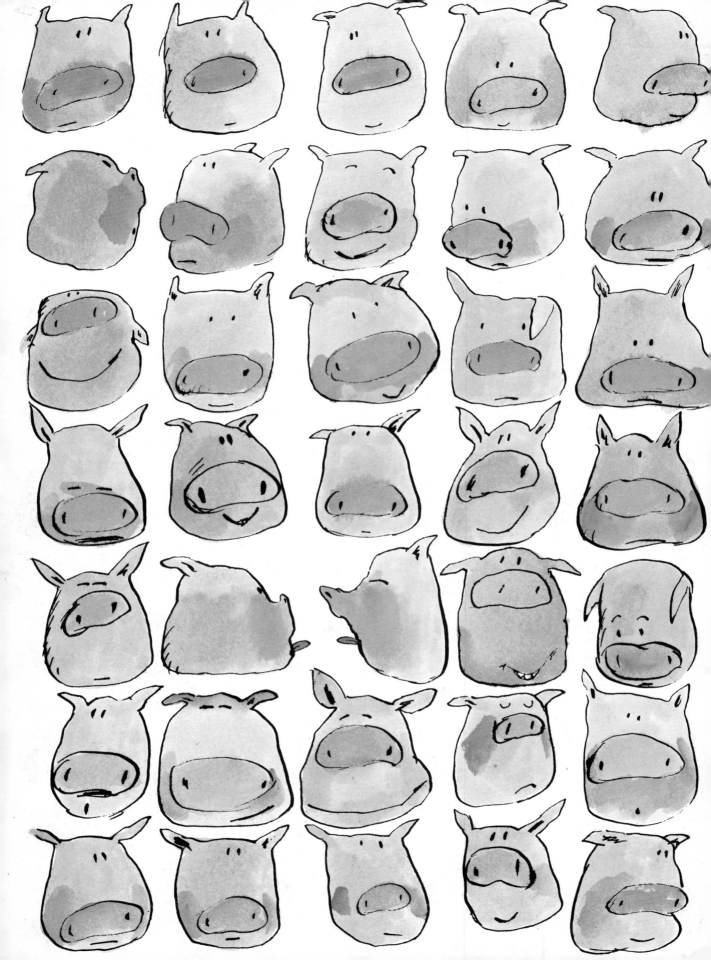

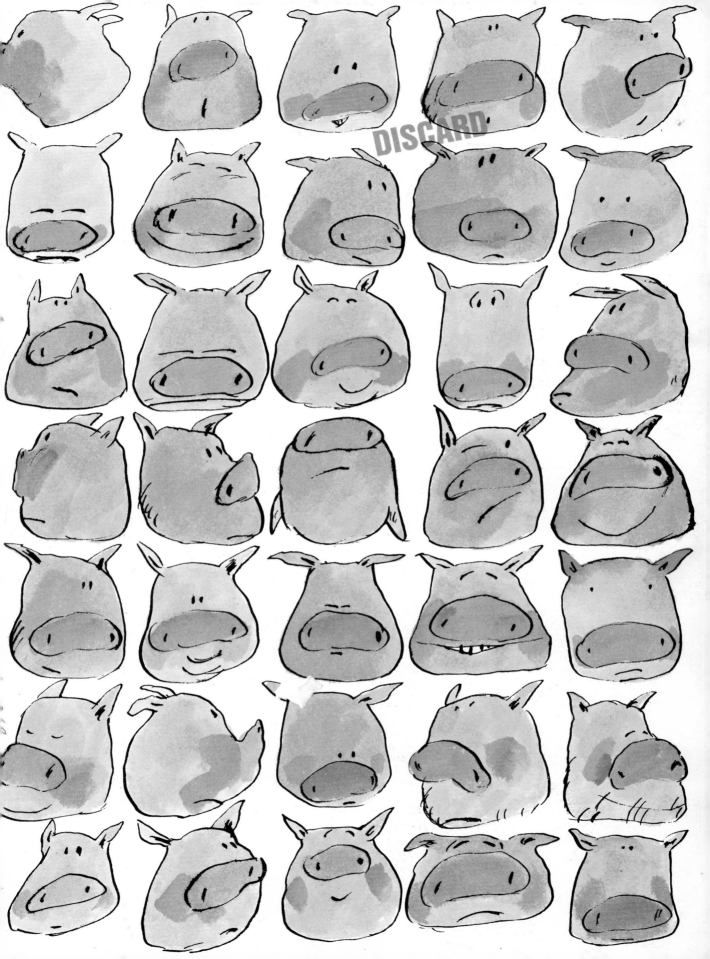

Library of Congress Cataloging in Publication Data. Ross, Tony. The three pigs. Summary: In this version of the traditional tale, the three little pigs leave a cramped high rise apartment in the city to cast their lots in the country. [1. Folklore. 2. Pigs—Fiction] I. Three little pigs. II. Title. III. Title: 3 pigs. PZ8.1.R693Th 1983 398.2'4529734 [E] 83-2356 ISBN 0-394-86143-4 ISBN 0-394-96143-9 (lib. bdg.) 10 9 8 7 6 5 4 3 2 1

THE THREE PIGS

by Tony Ross

PANTHEON BOOKS · NEW YORK

Pig and his two friends, Pig and Pig, lived on the 39th floor of a city building. Their apartment was cramped and too high, and the pigs felt sad and dizzy all the time.

"I know!" said Pig. "We'll move to the country."

"Yes!" said Pig and Pig.

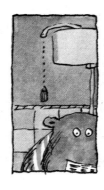

So the three pigs went to the bank to borrow money to buy a house, but the manager wouldn't lend them a penny. "We're not a *piggy bank*!" he said with a laugh.

"Then we'll build our own houses," said Pig.

"Yes!" agreed Pig and Pig. "One for each of us!"

The first pig met a man carrying a bundle of straw. He offered Pig some of the straw and Pig built a house with it. It wasn't strong, but it looked good and was soon finished.

But . . . a grey wolf lived near by.

"*Little pig, little pig, let me come in!*" said the wolf in a sweet voice.

But Pig was too smart to fall for that.

"*No, no,*" he said. "*Not by the hairs of my chinny-chin-chin!*"

"*Then . . .*" roared the wolf,

"...I'll huff and I'll puff, and I'll blow your house in!"
And he *did*.
And he gobbled Pig up.

Some friendly woodcutters gave the second pig some spare sticks.

"I'll build a house with these," he said, and went to find a pleasant spot.

When the house was finished, it was stronger than the house of straw, but still not all *that* strong.

In time, the same wolf came visiting.

"*Little pig, little pig, let me come in!*" said the wolf in a treacly voice.

But Pig was too smart for that.

"*No, no,*" he said. "*Not by the hairs of my chinny-chin-chin!*"

"*Then . . .*" roared the wolf,

"*. . . I'll huff and I'll puff, and I'll blow your house in!*"
And he *did*.
And he gobbled Pig up.

The third pig was smarter than the others. He found some help, and some bricks and cement, and built himself a real house. A strong one, with green woodwork.

In time, the grey wolf came calling.

"Little pig, little pig, let me come in!" wheedled the wolf.
"No, no," laughed Pig. *"Not by the hairs of my chinny-chin-chin!"*
"Then . . ." roared the wolf,

". . . I'll huff and I'll puff, and I'll blow your house in!"
And he huffed and he puffed, and he coughed and he wheezed, and he strained and he roared, but the house stood firm. So the wolf tried trickery.

"Meet me in the orchard tomorrow at six, and I'll help you collect apples," he said.

"Thank you," said Pig, but the next day he went to the orchard at five.

When the wolf arrived, Pig threw apples at him. As the wolf tripped over the apples, Pig darted home and bolted the door. He didn't forget, of course, to take a basket full of apples with him.

The wolf called on Pig again, trying hard to smile. "I'll take you to the fair tomorrow at eight," he offered.

"Thank you," said Pig, but next day he went to the fair at seven. When the wolf arrived, Pig jumped inside a milk can to hide. The can toppled over and clanked down the hill, straight for the terrified wolf.

When the wolf visited Pig later, he told him about the tin monster that had chased him away from the fair.

Pig laughed. "It was *me*, in my new milk can!"

The wolf was furious, and he stopped pretending to be the pig's friend. Snarling and spluttering, he clawed his way onto the roof and started to wriggle down the chimney.

Pig popped his largest pan onto the fire. It was full of boiling water and fresh celery.

With a snarl and a clatter, the wolf fell into the pot, and Pig slammed down the lid.

Two hours later, he gobbled the wolf up, with some asparagus tips and potato puffs.

With the wolf gone, it was quite safe to live in the country. More and more people moved from their apartments and built houses around Pig's house. Strong, brick houses.

Pig looked at the cramped and noisy streets. "Sometimes it feels like I am back on the 39th floor," he said with a sigh. "Oh, well, maybe I was just meant to be a city pig after all!"

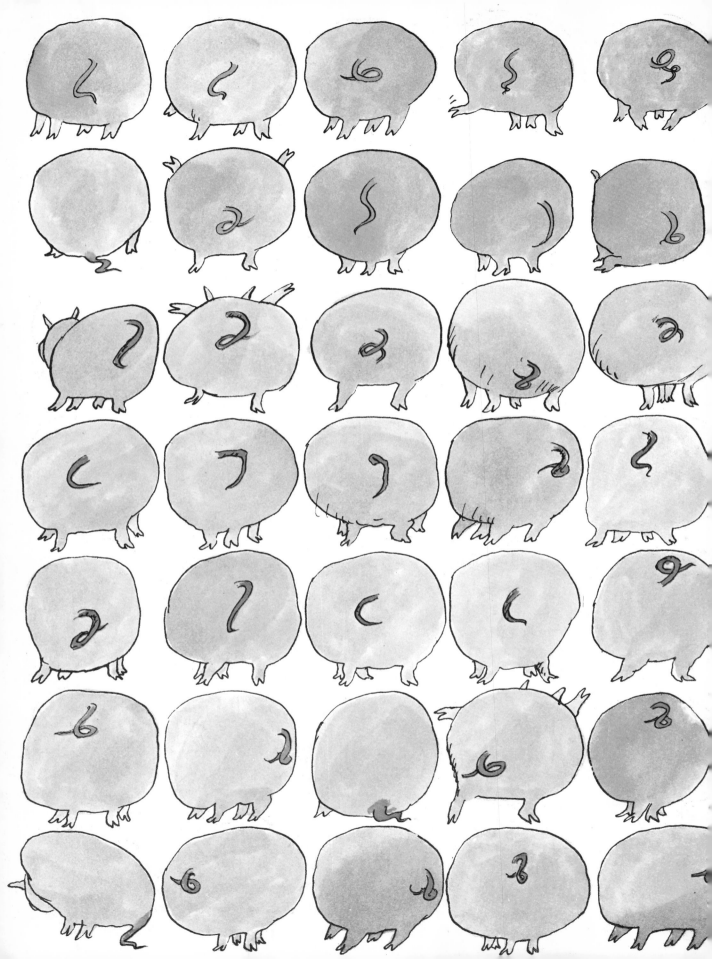

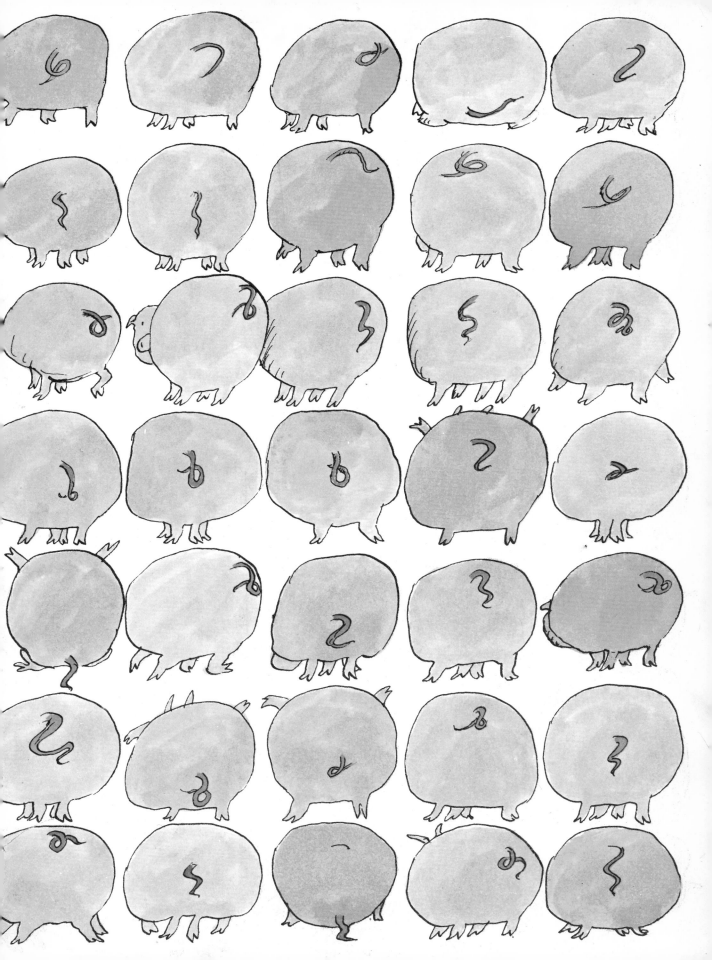